EARLY BIRD STORIES™

A Special Invitation

All Kinds of Religions

Lisa Bullard Illustrated by Holli Conger

LERNER PUBLICATIONS ◆ MINNEAPOLIS

NOTE TO EDUCATORS

Find text recall questions at the end of each chapter. Critical-thinking and text feature questions are available on page 23. These help young readers learn to think critically about the topic by using the text, text features, and illustrations.

Lerner Publications Company
An imprint of Lerner Publishing Group, Inc.
241 First Avenue North
Minneapolis, MN 55401 USA

For reading levels and more information, look up this title at www.lernerbooks.com.

Photos on p. 22 used with permission of: narikan/Shutterstock.com (kids volunteering); nisargmediaproductions/Shutterstock.com (Eid al-Fitr); Donna Ellen Coleman/Shutterstock.com (bat mitzvah).

Main body text set in Billy Infant.
Typeface provided by SparkyType.

Library of Congress Cataloging-in-Publication Data

Names: Bullard, Lisa, author. | Conger, Holli, illustrator.
Title: A special invitation : all kinds of religions / Lisa Bullard ; illustrated by Holli Conger.
Description: Minneapolis : Lerner Publications , 2022. | Series: All kinds of people (early bird stories) | Includes bibliographical references and index. | Audience: Ages 5-8 | Audience: Grades K-1 | Summary: "David visits his friend Zach's synagogue to celebrate his bar mitzvah. He keeps learning about his friends' religions and how to be respectful of them. Regardless of what you celebrate, we can celebrate one another"— Provided by publisher.
Identifiers: LCCN 2021010235 (print) | LCCN 2021010236 (ebook) | ISBN 9781728436937 (library binding) | ISBN 9781728438627 (paperback) | ISBN 9781728438290 (ebook)
Subjects: LCSH: Religions—Juvenile literature.
Classification: LCC BL92 .B844 2021 (print) | LCC BL92 (ebook) | DDC 200—dc23

LC record available at https://lccn.loc.gov/2021010235
LC ebook record available at https://lccn.loc.gov/2021010236

Manufactured in the United States of America
1-49654-49582-4/15/2021

TABLE OF CONTENTS

CHAPTER 1

A SPECIAL INVITATION

After playing baseball, my neighbor Zach invited me to his **bar mitzvah**. It's a Jewish celebration for his thirteenth birthday.

"What if I do something wrong?" I ask Dad.

"We just need to show **respect**, David," Dad says.

We go online to learn about being respectful at the **synagogue**.

It's fun to be part of Zach's special day! Zach reads in front of everyone in **Hebrew**.

✓ Check!
What is Zach celebrating?

CHAPTER 2

HELPING OTHERS

Sunday morning, Dad and I go to church.
"Is our religion called Lutheran?" I ask.

"It's **Christianity**," he says. "There are different kinds of Christianity, and Lutheran is one of them."

I like going to church.
I get to see friends
and **pray**.

I ask Dad if people of all religions pray.
“Not all religions pray, but a lot do,” he says.

My church volunteers at a place that serves people food. My friend Sophia is volunteering too.

I ask Sophia if she's there with her church.

She says she doesn't have a religion.

She's there to help people.

✓ Check! What does David do at church?

CHAPTER 3

MANY RELIGIONS

My friend Fahmi is at the park.
She's celebrating **Eid al-Fitr**.

It's a time for Muslims, people who practice Islam, to pray and come together.

Later, Kate comes over to babysit me. She says she's been learning about **Buddhism**.

✓ Check!
How is Eid al-Fitr celebrated?

It helps her stay peaceful. She's even calm when I throw my baseball in the house!

CHAPTER 4

GIVING THANKS

When Dad gets home, we say our prayers.

I give thanks for Dad, Zach, Sophia, Fahmi, and Kate. **And then I give thanks for baseball!**

✓ Check! How did David respect other people's religions?

LEARN ABOUT RELIGIONS

It's important to respect other people's religions. When people talk about their religion, listen with your ears and your heart.

Some people don't follow a religion. Every family has different values and beliefs.

A lot of people wear special clothes for their religion. Some Muslim girls and women wear a scarf called a hijab. Some Jewish people wear a cap called a kippah.

Eid al-Fitr celebrates the end of Ramadan. Ramadan is a month focused on prayer, fasting, and giving.

A boy's bar mitzvah and a girl's bat mitzvah are important Jewish ceremonies. They mark a passage into adulthood.

THINK ABOUT RELIGIONS:
CRITICAL-THINKING AND TEXT FEATURE QUESTIONS

Does your family follow a religion?

Why do you think some words in this book are bolded?

How do you respect other people's religions?

How does the glossary help you read this book?

GLOSSARY

bar mitzvah: a special celebration when a Jewish boy turns thirteen

Buddhism: a religion based on the teachings of Buddha

Christianity: a religion based on the teachings of Jesus Christ

religion: a system of faith

synagogue: a place where Jewish people meet for worship

volunteer: to do something helpful without being paid

LEARN MORE

Bullard, Lisa. ***Dress-Up Day: All Kinds of Clothes.*** Minneapolis: Lerner Publications, 2022.

Jones, Grace. ***Eid al-Fitr.*** New York: AV2, 2019.

URI Kids: World Religions
https://www.uri.org/kids/world-religions

INDEX